THE BLIND CONNEMARA

THE BLIND CONNEMARA

BY C. W. ANDERSON

COLLIER BOOKS
DIVISION OF MACMILLAN PUBLISHING CO., INC.
NEW YORK

COLLIER MACMILLAN PUBLISHERS
LONDON

Macmillan Publishing Co., Inc.
866 Third Avenue, New York, N.Y. 10022
Collier-Macmillan Canada Ltd., Toronto, Ontario

Library of Congress catalog card number: 76-158172

The Blind Connemara is published in a hardcover
edition by Macmillan Publishing Co., Inc.
Printed in the United States of America
First Collier Books Edition 1974

10 9 8 7 6 5 4 3 2 1

To Rhonda
and her blind Connemara,
"Pony"

CONTENTS

CONTENTS

THE BLIND CONNEMARA

1 THE GIRL WHO LOVED HORSES

The man in the brown riding breeches and leather puttees looked at the bay pony closely and put his hand under the mane.

"I wish all my riders would bring in their horses like that—nice and dry and not drawing a long breath. Gallop, gallop, gallop, that's all they know." There was just a hint of Irish brogue in the voice. "How did he go for you?"

"Oh, he's nice," said the girl. "Smooth and willing."

The man looked at her keenly. "He didn't pull at all?"

"Maybe a little at first," admitted the girl, "but I just let him ease himself and then he was fine."

"You have light hands," said the man, "and you really sit your horse. No balancing by the reins." He stopped and looked at her thoughtfully.

"Do you like children?" he asked. "Small children?"

"Yes," said the girl, "I do very much."

"Would you like to teach children to ride? I have more beginners on Saturday than I can handle. Would you care to try?"

"If you think I could, I'd love to," said the girl.

"I've been watching you since you've been riding here and I like the quiet way you handle a horse. You have good hands and a good seat, and what's more important you seem to understand horses. They're just like people—all are different. You seem to know that. And that's something you must try to teach— not just seat and hands. If a youngster has no idea of what a horse may do or why, he will never be a rider. Maybe he'll learn to stay on a horse but riding is a lot more than that."

Rhonda nodded.

"I'll leave it to you as to how you want to go ahead with the students. Some are quick and sure of themselves and want to gallop at once. Others are timid but if you go slowly with them they often turn out the best in the end. They're willing to listen and learn."

He looked over quickly and noticed how intently she listened.

"I'll see you Saturday at nine-thirty, then. Now about pay . . ."

"Please, Mr. Malley, could I take it out in rides? I'd rather do that."

"Fine. Take your pick any time. A ride by you would be good for a horse. Make him forget how some of the others yanked him around."

2 A PROBLEM HORSE

"I'm afraid I'll have to get rid of this one," said Mr. Malley one afternoon as Rhonda came into the stable.

"But he's such a nice-looking horse," said Rhonda.

"A lot of riders have had trouble with him," said Mr. Malley. "Yesterday he ran away with the Finchley girl and threw her. That sort of thing gives a riding stable a bad name. Still I hate to lose him. He's sound and has a nice conformation and is no trouble around the stable. It must be the way he's handled." He turned to her. "Would you take him out and tell me what you think? I've tried him around the ring and I can't find anything wrong with him. He's a little quick and eager and always up on the bit but that's all I could see."

"I'd like to," said Rhonda.

She walked into the stall and talked quietly to the little chestnut horse while she stroked his neck. Then she got a saddle and settled it carefully on his back before she tightened the girth.

"Snaffle or double bridle?" she asked.

"Maybe you'd better take the double bridle," said Mr. Malley. "He doesn't really need the curb—he has a light mouth—but he may still be on edge about what happened."

"Is there any special ride you want me to take him on?" she asked as she swung into the saddle and gathered up the reins.

"He ran away on the bridle path through the woods up there. Watch carefully and see if you can tell what set him off. Of course that girl isn't a real rider even though she thinks she is, and it might have been entirely her fault. But keep your eyes open and be careful."

The little chestnut went along smoothly and willingly until they came to the woods. Then she felt a tension building up in him. He kept looking from side to side suspiciously. Rhonda spoke to him quietly and soothingly but she still felt the tension. She stopped him and let him look around, for she knew if a horse saw things clearly he would not be nervous. It was only when he suddenly half-saw something that looked strange that he was frightened.

Then just ahead she saw what looked like a man crouching by the side of the path. Looking more closely, she soon realized it was only a blackened tree stump, but the horse was uneasy and did not want to go on. This must have been what frightened him yesterday. She must let him get a good look at it so that he would know what it was. But even when he was quite close he was still nervous. Not until he turned and faced the stump did he quiet down.

Rhonda dismounted and patted the horse soothingly, then led him up to the stump. She wanted to be very sure that he knew just what it was or he would always be frightened at that spot. Noticing how he turned his head to see the stump, she looked closely at his left eye.

It seemed bruised and half closed. He must have injured it and perhaps could see only dimly with it. That could explain everything! Probably he hadn't seen the stump until he turned his head and then it suddenly had seemed something terrifying.

When Rhonda got back to the stable she told Mr. Malley what she thought had happened.

He looked at the eye carefully and said, "You're right. That eye is in bad shape. It was bruised by a twig a while back but I thought it had cleared up. Some infection may have set in. I must get a vet to treat him. You can't have a horse with bad eyesight in your stable. It can cause real trouble. He only half-sees things and is easily frightened. You never know what will happen."

3   THE WHITE CONNEMARA

When Rhonda came to the stable a few days later
there was a horse van in front of it. She heard Mr.
Malley's voice call, "Easy, boy, easy." Then he came
down the sloping ramp leading the most beautiful pony
she had ever seen. He was shining white, his head was
high and his mane and tail were long and flowing. He
did not have the short legs and heavy short neck of the
average pony but looked like a small race horse, with
slim legs and arched neck.

"Would you take him for me, Rhonda?" Mr. Malley

called out. "Walk him around a little so he can stretch his legs. He's had a long ride in the van."

Rhonda gladly took the lead shank and led the pony away, talking to him and stroking him gently. He walked daintily beside her, blowing softly through his wide nostrils. His coat was like satin under her hand and after a few moments he turned and nuzzled her. She felt that he liked her and it made her very happy. She liked horses and always had, but her feeling for this pony was something different. Looking at him, she realized that he was all her dream horses in one and even more beautiful than she had ever imagined. As the van drove off, Mr. Malley came up to them.

"He's a nice pony, isn't he?" he said as he looked him over very carefully. "Mr. Strong bought him for his daughter. He's pure Connemara and one of the best I've ever seen."

"I've heard of them," said Rhonda. "What are they exactly?"

"They're an Irish breed of pony," said Mr. Malley, "noted for their intelligence and manners, and all of them can really jump. I've seen a fourteen-hand Connemara take a six-foot wall like nothing at all. And you never see a mean or stupid one. Mr. Strong had to pay plenty for this one."

Rhonda had been stroking the pony all the while and now he put his head against her shoulder.

"He seems to have taken to you," said Mr. Malley. "Would you mind grazing him out here for a while before we put him in his stall? It would ease him after his long ride."

"I'd love to," said Rhonda. "I think he's just wonderful—the most beautiful horse I have ever seen."

As the pony grazed, she continued studying him. He had such beautiful lines and moved with such lightness and grace that it was a pleasure just to look at him. He reminded her of pictures she had seen of Arabian horses: the same small muzzle with wide nostrils and a dark eye that was so large and intelligent.

She moved over beside him and laid her hand on his withers. As he felt her hand he raised his head and nuzzled her gently. A little thrill went through her. This was the way it was in her dreams. She had always wanted a pony of her own and often dreamed of horses: beautiful horses of unbelievable perfection. Her daydreams were much the same, but she had never been able to decide just what her perfect horse would look like. Now she knew!

When she led the white Connemara toward the stable she was very happy. Even though this wonderful pony was not her own she could see him every day, pat him and talk to him. Maybe Mr. Malley would let her groom him sometimes.

After he was in his stall Rhonda found a soft cloth and rubbed the pony down thoroughly and gently, talking to him quietly. She always talked to horses. They seemed to like it, and with this lovely pony it was like talking to a friend. There was such awareness in his look that she felt he understood everything.

When finally she had to go he turned and whinnied.

"He doesn't want you to go," said Mr. Malley, who had just come in. "He really likes you."

"I think he's wonderful," said Rhonda. "Could I help take care of him sometime?"

"Anytime at all," said Mr. Malley. "You're my best stable boy."

4   A TOP PONY

The white Connemara was cantering around the ring. Two jumps had been set up, one on each side of the ring. Mr. Strong stood leaning on the fence with Mr. Malley, watching the pony intently.

"Did you ever see a smoother action, Tim?" asked Mr. Strong. "He just seems to float along."

"He's really something," said Tim Malley. "One of the best I ever saw. Miss Sally should win plenty of ribbons with him."

"What are the jumps at?" asked Mr. Strong.

"Three-six," said Tim Malley. "That's all they ask for in the pony classes. But if he's like the rest of the Connemaras another foot or even two wouldn't bother him. They can usually jump fences that will stop most horses."

Sally Strong swung him toward the first jump and he sailed over it like a bird in flight. He put on a little speed coming to the next jump and soared over it with a foot to spare.

"That's beautiful," said Mr. Strong. "He's a natural jumper if I ever saw one. He could take any outside course in style."

He turned to Tim Malley. "He's only entered in the pony classes at the Woodvale Show. Do you think we should try him against the horses?"

"I wouldn't at first," said Tim Malley. "Let him get the feel of things. Don't push him. There are a lot of nice ponies around, and a blue against them wouldn't be a pushover. There's plenty of time to go on from there."

Sally rode over to them. She looked pleased and excited. "Wasn't he fine?" she said. The pony came to Rhonda and nuzzled her.

"Hello, Rhonda," said Sally. "He seems to know you."

"She helped me to unload him and put him away

when he came," said Tim Malley. "They seemed to take to each other right away."

Mr. Strong turned to Rhonda. "You really love horses, don't you? I've noticed the way you handle them."

"Yes, I do," said Rhonda. "More than anything."

"It seems to come through to them," said Mr. Strong. "They all go well for you. You don't have a horse of your own?"

Rhonda shook her head. "Maybe someday, I hope."

"Would you raise the jumps?" Sally asked Tim Malley. "I'd like to try him at four feet."

"Sure thing," he said. "He'll take them the same. Maybe a foot more." He went into the ring and raised the bars on the standards.

"There you are," he said. "Four feet, even."

The white Connemara galloped toward the first one gaily and eagerly, his ears pricked and his tail a flag. His take-off was so smooth and effortless that he seemed as much in his element in the air as on the ground. He cleared the bar in a wide arc, landed softly and galloped on. He rose to the next jump in the same soaring flight, and was over the bar with inches to spare.

"It's a pleasure to watch him after seeing all the horses that have been schooled long and hard over the jumps. He does it so easily you begin to wonder just what he could do if you pushed him."

"It's best not to try to find out," said Tim Malley. "With a pony like this, he's probably never made a mistake or had a fall. Now he feels he can do anything. Better keep it that way."

5   RHONDA RIDES THE WHITE CONNEMARA

When Rhonda came to the stable Tim Malley was outside mounting two girl riders and checking their tack. She went into the stable and directly to the white Connemara's stall. He whinnied softly when he saw her.

"Hello, Pony," she said as she patted him. "How are you?" The pony rubbed against her.

"I thought I'd find you here," said Tim Malley, who had just come in.

Rhonda turned to him eagerly. "I couldn't get over to the Woodvale Show," she said. "How did he go?"

"Wonderfully," said Tim Malley. "You just couldn't fault him. After the judges got a good look at him they didn't have eyes for anything else. And you couldn't blame them. After him the others were just ponies; you know, sort of short and choppy in their gaits. He moves like a little race horse, smooth and flowing."

"And his jumping?" asked Rhonda.

"He just floated over. He had the crowd cheering all the way."

"So he won," said Rhonda.

"Every class he was entered in," said Tim Malley. "There were some nice ponies there too but they were just outclassed."

"What do they plan to do now?" asked Rhonda.

"I suggested they try the best: the Westwood Show next month. The top ponies in this part of the country will be entered and there are several good Connemaras too. A blue ribbon there would really mean something."

"And you think he can do it?" asked Rhonda anxiously. "Of course I think nothing can beat him but what do you really think?"

"If he goes as he did Saturday nothing can beat him. You can't be better than perfect."

The Westwood Show was a week away and Rhonda waited for it eagerly. Mr. Strong had invited Mr.

Malley and her to ride over with him. She saw the white Connemara every day and often she groomed him if Mr. Malley was busy. He seemed to watch for her now and always whinnied as soon as he saw her or heard her voice.

Today Tim Malley greeted her with a broad smile. "I've got a little job for you today if you don't mind," he said. "Mr. Strong called and said that Sally couldn't come over to ride today and he felt the pony should get some exercise as the rain kept him in yesterday. He wondered if you would take him out."

Rhonda was in seventh heaven. She was actually going to ride the white Connemara! In a daze she went and got a saddle and bridle. Never had she been so careful to see that the saddle fitted perfectly or the bridle was adjusted so that the bit fitted lightly in the pony's mouth. When she mounted she felt so happy and lighthearted. This was a day of days. When she felt the light springy stride as they started, she was sure it must still be a dream.

Rhonda was actually going to ride the white Connemara!
When she felt the light springy stride as they started,
she was sure it must still be a dream.

They were coming back along the bridle trail through the woods and the Connemara's trot was long and swinging and unbelievably smooth. Just ahead she saw a boy with a dog in the path. They quickly dodged into the bushes when they saw her coming. She knew it wasn't good for them to be there. It could frighten a horse if he didn't know they were there and saw them suddenly. But she was sure the pony had seen them and would watch for them. She patted his neck and found he was calm and relaxed.

When they came to the bushes she saw that the boy was holding the dog by the collar. The dog gave a sharp bark, and the Connemara shied into the bushes. Rhonda soothed him with hand and voice but he was all upset.

He had been surprised to see them there! And yet Rhonda felt sure he must have seen them. Any horse would. He quieted down quickly but Rhonda was thoughtful all the way back to the stable. It was all a little strange.

6   A BOY'S BLIND PONY

Rhonda sat beside Mr. Strong as they drove along on the way to the Westwood Horse Show. Sally had decided to ride over with some of her friends.

"Did you enjoy your ride on our pony the other day?" asked Mr. Strong. "Did he go well?"

"He was wonderful, just wonderful," said Rhonda. "I never felt anything so smooth. Even his walk is different—so springy."

"That's the way he looks," said Mr. Strong. "He'll have to be at his best today. There are some very fine ponies entered." He looked over at her. "You seem sort of serious. Is something on your mind?"

"It's really nothing, probably," said Rhonda. "But I keep thinking about it." She told him of the boy and dog on the bridle path in the woods.

"You were close enough to see them clearly?" he asked when she had finished.

"Oh yes," she said. "I felt sure the pony did too, but it seems he didn't. I can't quite understand why and it keeps bothering me."

Mr. Strong was serious and thoughtful for a while. "I'll get a vet to check his eyes when we get back. Good eyes are absolutely essential to a horse. One with any defect is a risky thing. A horse can panic if he doesn't see things clearly."

He was silent for a long time.

"When I was a boy I had a pony I loved very much," he said at last. "He began to go blind when I'd had him about a year. At first I couldn't believe it; I just wouldn't believe it. But finally I had to. He was almost bumping into things and going very uncertainly as if he were feeling his way. All his smooth trot and canter were gone. The vet father called in wanted him put away. He said a blind horse was dangerous to ride. If he were frightened and ran away he might crash into a wall or a building. But I couldn't bear to lose him. So finally he said that if I were patient enough to get the pony to trust me completely it might work. He explained to me that I would have to be the pony's eyes—tell him what was ahead and always look out for him and tell him what to do.

"We finally made it," continued Mr. Strong. "In time he went as freely as any pony and most people didn't realize he was blind. He even won ribbons in small shows—just walk, trot and canter of course. I couldn't ask him to jump something he couldn't see. He might even have learned to do that but it seemed too much to ask."

"That was wonderful," said Rhonda, her eyes shining. "It must have taken a long time."

"Months and months. He had to learn 'up' and 'down' and 'careful' and to be absolutely sure I was always looking out for him. You can imagine what it was like for him to move boldly and confidently in complete darkness. He had to trust me completely and be as sure of my using my eyes for him as he once was of his own sight. That took a lot of time but it was worth it. I think that pony was more devoted to me than ever a horse was to anybody. He depended on me and was never happy when I was away. I've never forgotten him."

"You must have loved him very much."

"I did. And I'm sure he knew it. He would do anything at all for me without question.

"But about our pony," said Mr. Strong. "I don't think it's all that serious. He may have been looking at something else so that he didn't see the boy and dog. Still I'll have a vet check his eyes right away just to be sure."

7   SOMETHING VERY WRONG

The show grounds were full of horses and ponies.

"This is really a big show," said Mr. Strong. "There must be fifty ponies here, some of them pretty nice. Winning here is going to take a little doing."

As they looked around they saw Tim Malley leading the white Connemara. He came over to them.

"There will be some big classes," he said. "It looks as if everybody in the state with a pony is here. Where's Miss Sally?"

"She's driving over with some friends. She should be here any minute."

"I hope so," said Tim Malley. "This pony is not quite himself. Sort of nervous and jittery. I'd like her to hack him around a little and see if he won't settle down."

As he walked away Rhonda noticed the way the pony looked around quickly, startled at everything.

"He certainly is upset," said Mr. Strong. "I've never seen him like this before."

Then a voice called over the loud-speaker, "Riders at the gate for Class One: Ponies Under Saddle."

"Where can Sally be?" said Mr. Strong. "She's in this class and they won't wait for anyone with all the entries they've got."

He turned to Rhonda. "Will you take him until she comes? We don't want to miss this class. It was made to order for him. Walk, trot and canter and two three-foot jumps. It should be just play for him."

When Rhonda was mounted she felt something was different. The pony seemed uncertain and hesitant and he did not step out in his usual bold way. She was looking around for Mr. Malley to ask him about it when her number was called. She turned him toward the gate, hoping it was only her imagination.

In the ring she started him around at a trot at the

ringmaster's order. It wasn't at all the trot she had gotten from him the day she had ridden him. Gone was the floating action, the beautiful rhythm of stride. It was as if he were unsure of his footing or what was before him. She tried to soothe him with hand and voice but she could not get rid of the tension she felt in him. When a canter was called for it was the same: the pony's stride was short, choppy and uncertain. Rhonda was very upset but there seemed nothing that she could do. The pony just wasn't himself.

Now it was her turn to jump. Rhonda was worried but she put him into a canter toward the first fence. As they approached it she felt his uncertainty even more strongly, and just when she thought he would take off he swerved to the left, narrowly missing the standard. A refusal! She had never thought to see the day that this wonderful pony would refuse a jump. Turning him back a half-dozen strides, she again sent him at the jump. He got in too close, hit the top bar and sent it flying. The judge waved them out of the ring.

Rhonda was close to tears when she rode back to where Mr. Strong and Tim Malley waited.

"Don't feel too badly, Rhonda," said Mr. Strong. "It wasn't your fault. Something is wrong with him."

Just then Sally came up. "We had a breakdown

and were held up," she said. "What's happened?" she asked as she saw the expression on their faces.

Mr. Strong told her. Her jaw tightened and a stubborn look came on her face as she listened.

"Something is wrong with him—very wrong. We might as well take him home and I'll get a vet to check him over."

"I told my friends I was coming home with a handful of blue ribbons and I'm not going back empty-handed," said Sally. "Wait till I get a riding crop," and she strode off.

"Number 36," called the announcer and Sally rode into the ring. The white pony was clearly very nervous and moved quickly but uncertainly. Sally's jaw was set and her tension showed in the way she handled the pony. His mouth was open under the pressure of the bit. She knew what he could do and saw no reason why he should not do it now. She had ridden ponies who sometimes became stubborn and contrary, and clearly she thought this was the case here.

The white pony circled the ring at trot and canter as he had for Rhonda, not stubbornly with ears laid back but uncertainly, often shortening stride as if he saw some obstacle ahead.

When the ringmaster called for the jumps she turned

him toward the first one and gave him several sharp cuts with the crop. He galloped toward the fence uncertainly. When he felt the crop again he put on speed and jumped. He was too far away by a full stride and although he jumped very big it was not enough. He crashed on top of the fence and went to his knees. Sally flew over his head, putting out a hand to break her fall. The pony scrambled to his feet, looking very startled. Sally got up slowly, holding her right arm, a grimace of pain on her face.

8   THE END OF THE ROAD?

Rhonda's sleep was fitful and disturbed that night. She brooded over the white Connemara as if he were her own. Early the next morning she went over to the riding stable. Mr. Strong was there. He was talking to a man outside the Connemara's stall.

"It's a shame with such a beautiful pony," he said. "But there is no hope for him. He will see less and less and very soon he will be completely blind. I'm afraid there is nothing to do but put him away."

"There's no hope for a cure?" asked Mr. Strong.

"None at all. Everything has been tried for that ailment and nothing works."

Mr. Strong and the veterinarian went out of the stable. Rhonda's eyes smarted with tears when she went into the Connemara's stall. She put her arms around his neck and hugged him hard as the tears came.

After a long while she heard Mr. Strong speak in a gentle voice. "I know how you feel, Rhonda," he said. "It was like that with me when they told me my pony was going blind. It seemed like the end of the world."

"What will you do now?" she asked, lifting her tear-stained face.

"I suppose there is nothing to do but put him down as the vet suggested," said Mr. Strong. "He's not a safe ride now and it will be worse as time goes on."

"But remember what you told me about your own pony when you were a boy."

"You have no idea of the time and patience it took," said Mr. Strong. "I had to be his eyes and never forget for a moment. If he had had a single stumble or a fall because I forgot to warn him it would have been all off. I couldn't make a single mistake. He had to be absolutely sure before he could trust me completely and step out boldly in complete darkness."

"But how about Sally?" asked Rhonda.

"Sally likes horses but not quite like that," said Mr. Strong. "She wants things now—not tomorrow. Most of her friends are like that." He stopped and looked at her very seriously. "You really love this pony, don't you? Even though he isn't yours."

Rhonda stroked the Connemara's neck. "A pony like this," she said, "so beautiful, so wonderful—you don't have to own him to love him."

"If you could have him, would you be willing to take the time to work with him, gain his complete confidence, really see for him? It would take months—maybe a year or more."

"Oh yes," said Rhonda, her heart beating fast. "I wouldn't mind how long it took. I love to be with him. He's like a person."

"One thing will help in gaining his confidence," continued Mr. Strong. "He still has some vision although it is greatly impaired. When you warn him of something ahead and he finally sees it for himself, it will make him realize that you are really looking out for him. But you must always be alert, always remember he lives in a world of darkness and by himself would scarcely dare to move in any direction. You must never relax or daydream when you are riding him, but warn him of every hole or rock or root in the road that might make him stumble. With voice and rein and knee you can do this. Soon he will learn from your voice whether 'up' is high or just a small ridge, and whether 'down' is a steep bank or just a little slope.

"If you go ahead with this as I think you will, you'll be closer to your horse than anyone will believe possible. For this is no common pony. I looked over dozens before I chose him. He had everything, not only conformation but disposition and intelligence. If you can be his eyes for him it's still all there."

9   A HORSE OF HER OWN

She had a horse of her own! Something she had always wanted. A beautiful horse, the most wonderful horse she had ever seen. The fact that he would soon be blind did not worry her. She felt sure it would make no difference. All it would take was patience and affection and she had both in abundance.

Tim Malley was very sympathetic and offered to board the pony in exchange for her teaching children on Saturdays. He had some doubts about how effective training could really be in such a case—in his experience a blind horse was always put down—but in the face of her enthusiasm he concealed them.

Watching Rhonda in the stall stroking the white pony and talking to him softly, he thought to himself, "If it's possible, if it can be done, this girl is the one to do it."

A little later he saw her lead the Connemara from the stable.

"Not riding?" he asked.

"Not for a day or two," she said. "That fall at the show must have been a shock for him, the kind of jumper he really is. I doubt if it ever happened to him before. I want him to forget about it. I'll just walk him around and let him graze. I want to find out just how much he can still see. I think I can do that better if I walk beside him."

Watching as they walked away, Tim Malley noticed how closely the pony walked beside the girl. "He certainly trusts her," he thought, "and that could take them far. They might make it."

As she looked at the white pony, Rhonda again marveled at the balance and the perfect proportion— nothing too much, nothing too little. She could see nothing that she would wish changed. That this shining thing was her own was almost more than she could comprehend. To her this was not a horse with a flaw that had been cast aside. He was still perfection, only temporarily impaired by misfortune. She knew, deep inside herself, that this pony would again be what he had been.

She heard riders on the nearby road. The pony heard them too and raised his head and looked about. The riders came from behind the trees and approached, but it was clear to her that the pony did not see them. Rhonda, watching carefully, realized that he saw them only when they were a short distance away, and perhaps then only dimly. His eyesight was going fast. She realized she must do everything possible to teach him commands while he could still see enough to realize what she was doing. It would be easier now than when he was in total darkness.

She led him toward the road. When they came to a small ditch, she stopped to make sure he saw it, then said "down" and led him ahead. On the other side she said "up," making the word very clear and distinct. They went across the road and toward a very narrow gap in a stone wall. She stopped to let the pony see how narrow the space was. Then she led him through, saying "Easy now, easy." She knew how brushing

She stopped to let the pony see
how narrow the space was. Then she led him through,
saying "Easy now, easy."

against something could upset a horse and it was very important for him to be quiet and obedient at such times.

As they went across the field, she tried to make her voice indicate what the ground was like. "Down" in a low voice for a small decline, "up" in the same tone if it was only a ridge where he must pick up his feet a little higher. Since the pony could still see the terrain, she felt he would relate her commands and the tone of her voice to what was before him.

She knew horses had an amazing memory, that they never forgot a spot where something had happened. Sometimes on a ride she was surprised when a horse grew tense or nervous, until she realized that he was remembering something that had frightened him a long time before. Perhaps a partridge had flown up just there with that feathery thunder that was so startling.

When they got back to the stable Rhonda felt they had made a good start. It seemed to her that the pony lifted his feet a little higher at her "up" without even looking. Her heart was light. It was going to work! She knew it would.

10   EYES FOR TWO

In the weeks that passed the Connemara's eyesight grew worse very rapidly. Now he depended almost entirely on Rhonda's signals to him. If he saw at all it was so dimly that it only made him uncertain. But her voice seemed to reassure him. "Everything is fine now," she would say, even if she knew he did not understand. She felt that somehow he gained confidence from her tone and knew she was looking out for him so that he could go ahead with complete assurance. She found that if she saw a dog ahead on a path where they were riding, in some strange way the pony was prepared when they approached the dog and was not nervous. She knew he understood only a few words but nevertheless she felt that her thoughts were communicated to him. And as his eyesight failed, his hearing seemed to become even more acute. He almost seemed to get an echo from obstacles. Rhonda was sure that he did.

One day she was riding him around in the ring. He was going at a slow canter, rocking along in the most beautiful rhythm with not the slightest hesitation. After the first time around he seemed to have the dimensions in his mind and he went along on a loose rein lap after lap.

"Wonderful!" came a voice from the rail. "That just couldn't be better. I don't know how you did it, Rhonda, but no one would ever guess he was blind."

Rhonda pulled up and rode over to Tim Malley, who had come up and watched them.

"He goes as well as he ever did," he said. "I would never have believed a blind pony could go like that. Why don't you show him in one of the 4H shows? Just 'walk, trot and canter.' He would be hard to beat the way he goes now."

"But wouldn't the judge consider a blind pony unsound?" asked Rhonda.

"I don't think so," said Tim Malley. "Not when he goes like that. It seems to me he ought to give him an extra ribbon for doing what he does with such a handicap."

When she came to the stable next morning, Tim Malley called her over and pointed to a poster on the wall.

"Here's the perfect spot for your pony," he said.

"4H Show for the Benefit of the Sanders Home for Crippled Children," she read.

"Think what it might do for those youngsters who are crippled to see what a blind pony can do," said Tim Malley. "It will really mean something to them."

"I'd like to do it. I'll try to get Pony ready to do his best," said Rhonda.

"Fine," said Tim Malley. "I'll pass the word around. It isn't every day you see a blind horse able to do what this one does. I'll let the papers know about it."

11   THE BLIND CONNEMARA
MAKES THE HEADLINES

The next day Rhonda was working the white pony in the ring when she saw a photographer come up with another man and Tim Malley. They came over to her and Tim Malley said, "These men are from the *Portersville Sentinel* and they'd like pictures and a story about you and your pony."

"But he's just a pony," said Rhonda, flustered. "What can there be for a story?"

"But he's blind, isn't he?" said one man. "And Tim Malley tells me he goes as confidently as a horse that can see. Didn't that take a lot of work and training?"

"I suppose it did," said Rhonda slowly. "I just loved the pony so I never thought about that. But he is sort of wonderful, the way he understands and trusts me."

"And what do you do exactly?" asked the man.

"I try to imagine how it would be for me if I were blind, and I try to tell him how everything is. He knows 'up' and 'down' and 'careful' and things like that, but I feel I can tell him more than that by talking to him. Maybe he doesn't understand the words but somehow things get through to him. Maybe it's just the sound of the voice or the way I say it, but I know when I say 'this is nice smooth going' he really goes along at his best trot and canter, and if I say 'this is a little rough so pick up your feet' he goes quite differently. Of course I may also signal a little through the reins or knees without realizing it, but I feel it's mostly the voice he goes by."

"And what do you call him?" asked the man.

"Just 'Pony,'" said Rhonda. "That's what I called him before I knew what his name was and he seemed to like it, so I've always just called him that."

"Could we get a few pictures of you and the pony?" asked the man. "The paper would like to give the show a little publicity and you two are the special attraction, we think."

The photographer came into the ring and snapped several pictures of the pony trotting and cantering and then asked Rhonda to dismount and stand beside the pony.

"What do you want us to do?" asked Rhonda. The pony pushed his head over to nuzzle her and ask for affection.

"Hold that," said the man. "That's perfect."

As the time for the show approached the white pony seemed almost to be aware of it, for his trot and canter became even smoother and more beautifully rhythmic. Never had Rhonda felt such a flow of effortless movement. His gaits had always seemed to her the ultimate in smoothness and grace but now they seemed to go even beyond that.

When she came to the stable a day before the show, she found Tim Malley reading a paper and looking very pleased.

As the time for the show approached the white pony seemed almost to be aware of it, for his trot and canter became even smoother and more rhythmic.

"You and the Connemara are sort of famous," he said. "Take a look at this. They really did a nice job on it." There were pictures of her and the pony under headlines that read, "Blindness No Handicap to Pony."

"Read it," he said. "For once they got it all down right."

She read: "Miss Rhonda Wallis has a beautiful white pony, a Connemara, which is a famous Irish breed. The pony was given to her when he went blind. Tim Malley, a veteran horseman who runs the stable where the pony is boarded, says that always in his experience a blind horse is put away since he can panic and cause a bad accident. But this is something else again. The pony trusts Rhonda completely. She is literally his eyes and he knows it. He steps out in complete confidence and moves so freely that no one would know he was blind. But in a way he does see. She tells him 'up' and 'down' and more than that. She tries to give him a feeling of things by her voice. And there is no doubt that in some strange way it all comes through to him. For no horse could gallop with such gaiety and freedom if he did not feel absolutely certain of what was before him.

"Rhonda says, 'I talk to him to make him feel I am always watching out for him—never forgetting him.

That's very important. He depends on me. I must never make a mistake.'

"This is an unusual horse and a most unusual girl. It is appropriate that they should make their first appearance since the pony went blind in this show for the benefit of the Sanders Home for Crippled Children. It should give these children a great lift to see such a fine performance from a pony who is handicapped so severely that he was considered useless."

12   THE SHOW RING AGAIN

The Sanders Home children had a section to themselves and Rhonda saw them at once. There were
wheelchairs and youngsters on crutches. She rode
over to introduce herself and let them see the white
Connemara. Their eyes grew big as they looked at
him.

"Is he really blind?" asked one boy. "He moves as
if he could see everything."

"I try to tell him what everything is like and he
seems to understand," said Rhonda. "He knows I
look out for him and he trusts me."

"He's so beautiful," said a little girl in a wheel chair. "I hope he wins all the prizes."

When the class was called Rhonda rode into the ring and circled it once to give the pony an idea of its size. She knew this was important, for once he had the size in his mind he scarcely needed the reins to make the circle exactly.

Most of the other ponies in the class were smaller, more of the Shetland type, and their gaits were rather short and choppy compared to the longer, smoother stride of the Connemara. Rhonda felt that her pony really stood out. She stole a quick look at the judge, a gray-haired man, and saw how intently he was watching her pony. Now she knew it wasn't her imagination. That smoothness of movement under her was really there.

When the canter was called for, some of the ponies scurried along at a gallop as if it were to be a race. But the white pony rocked in the rhythm that Rhonda knew and loved, heedless of the ponies galloping around him. This time when she looked at the judge there was no doubt in her mind—the look on his face was unmistakably one of approval.

Finally the ringmaster asked them to line up. Rhonda was very happy. She knew from what she had

seen that her pony ranked very high in the judge's estimation and she could not see that any other pony had come close to equaling his performance. But then her heart sank! They were moving a jump into the middle of the ring. She had had no idea a jump would be called for in this class.

She rode up to the judge and said, "Sir, is a jump called for in this class?"

"Yes, it is," he said. "But it's only two and a half feet. That shouldn't bother such a pony as yours."

"But, sir," said Rhonda, "this pony is blind. I could never ask him to jump something he can't see. I didn't know a jump was called for."

"This pony is blind?" exclaimed the judge. "I can't believe it! He goes so boldly and freely. He is one of the finest ponies I have ever seen. How did you do it?"

He seemed so sympathetic and understanding that Rhonda told him everything that had happened.

"I wish I could give you the blue but I have to follow the rules," said the judge. "But I am going to explain

When the class was called Rhonda rode
into the ring and circled it once
to give the pony an idea of its size.

to everyone here why it is that the best pony does not win. That I can do."

After the jumping was over and the ribbons awarded, the judge's voice came over the loud-speaker.

"I want to explain why the white Connemara, which was the best pony in this class, did not get a ribbon. He is blind, and his owner, Miss Rhonda Wallis, did not know a jump was called for in this class. She feels that to ask him to jump something he cannot see is asking too much. Except for this he would have won, for I would never have known he was blind by his performance. It was one of the best I have seen. To do what he has done with such a handicap calls for special praise, beyond a mere ribbon."

13   THE BLIND PONY JUMPS

Tim Malley was very sympathetic when Rhonda told him of the show.

"I didn't know that those pony classes called for a jump," he said. "I should have looked it up. I'm sorry. But still, for the judge to have made that announcement was nice. And coming from him especially. He's one of the best."

"I didn't really mind too much," said Rhonda. "The children were more upset than I was. They all thought Pony was wonderful and they found it hard to understand why he didn't win. I would have liked to win for them. Maybe some other time."

Rhonda was trotting the white Connemara around the ring. There were two other ponies there and they were taking a small jump set up in the center of the ring. Rhonda noticed that Pony cocked his ears and listened as the riders urged their ponies on. He kept pulling toward the jump but Rhonda could not understand why. Finally, when the other ponies left, she let him go over to the jump. He seemed to sense when he got to it, and put his nose down to feel the height of the bar. Perhaps he was curious to know how high they were jumping. She remembered how gaily he had jumped before blindness came on him. It hadn't been an effort. He had been like something with wings. She supposed some of that feeling might still be there, even in darkness.

Then suddenly she felt him gather himself and tense his muscles. She barely had time to tighten her knee grip before she felt the thrust as he leaped. He was

She barely had time to tighten her knee grip
before she felt the thrust as he leaped.
He was over the bar with a foot to spare.

over the bar with a foot to spare. A joyous thrill ran through her. So it was still there, that love of jumping. Even when he couldn't see he couldn't resist it. All he had to know was what was before him and how high it was. Pony cantered gaily and proudly around the ring, then pulled again toward the center. He wanted to jump again. As before, he came up to the jump and put his nose down, then moved back half a stride and sailed over the bar easily.

"You're wonderful, Pony, just wonderful!" said Rhonda, patting his neck.

"That's right," said Tim Malley, who was leaning on the rail. "You won't need to worry about a jump in any of the classes next time. He hasn't forgotten a thing. He's still a natural jumper and almost back to where he started from. It's as if he can still see."

He paused and watched the white pony nuzzling Rhonda.

"And in a way he can. You do that for him and he knows it. That's why he moves so freely and boldly. I never in my life expected to see a blind horse do what he does. But he's a most unusual pony, and you— you're different too."

Rhonda felt the directness and honesty of the compliment and was flattered.

"I love the pony and it's not a job to work with him. He's so wonderful, so trusting and brave and gay. He tries so hard to do everything he ever did and I think he almost does."

14   THE CHILDREN'S HERO

The next morning Rhonda found a letter by her
breakfast plate. Looking at the back she saw it was
from the Sanders Home for Crippled Children. Open-
ing it she read:

"The children who were at the 4H Horse Show all
want me to thank you for being so kind in letting them
see and get acquainted with your wonderful pony.
They have talked of little else since then and were
heartbroken that he did not win. They felt it was
unfair to expect a blind pony to jump an obstacle that

he could not see. But they still think he must be the most wonderful pony in the world to go the way he does, so gaily and surely, when he is blind.

"They made me promise to take them to the next show where he appears. We have a large bus at our service, so unless the distance is very great I am sure we could make it.

"We of the staff want to thank you so much for your kindness and consideration toward these handicapped children. Such things mean much more to them than to most children. If you would be so kind as to let us know when next these children might have a chance to see their hero we would be very grateful.

"Very sincerely,

"Jane Harris

"The Sanders Home for Crippled Children"

Immediately after breakfast Rhonda sat down to answer the letter. She wrote:

"It was a pleasure to show my pony to the children for I could see at once how they felt about him. I love the pony and when I see someone else who feels as I do about him it makes me very happy.

"Please tell the children that the next time they need not worry when a jump is called for. Yesterday in the ring at the stable he heard some ponies jumping and got very excited. When they left the ring he insisted on going over to the jump. He felt the height with his nose and before I realized what he intended to do he gathered himself and jumped over it—way over it. Then he did it again, even higher. He used to be a wonderful jumper and now I realize his spirit and desire for the feeling of it are still there. All he needs to know is how high the jump is.

"The judge at the show was very kind in announcing that except for the jumping my pony would have won, so I think you can promise the children that the next time he will win.

"I think we will try for the Tri-State 4H Show next month at Northwood. It's an important show and there will be some pretty fine ponies there, but Pony is going so beautifully now that I feel he can do it. We have to keep to classes that have only a single jump, because he has to walk up to it and feel its height and then jump from a standstill. I will let you know the time of the class he will compete in as soon as I am certain of it.

"It will be a pleasure to see the children again and I will make sure they all get a good close look at Pony and can pat him if they wish to.

"Most sincerely,

"Rhonda Wallis"

15 THE BLIND
CONNEMARA FUND

Every day after a ride, whether just in the ring or across country, Rhonda always finished up with a couple of jumps in the ring. Now that she had made a promise to the children she wanted to be doubly sure that Pony was at his very best for the Tri-State Show. Each day the white pony took the jump with a little more enthusiasm and she soon realized he looked forward to it.

There was great interest in the white pony in the

whole countryside. The story in the newspaper had stirred everybody's sympathy and everywhere that Rhonda rode people wished her luck. They had often seen this girl and the white pony along the roads, but they had never realized that the pony that went so beautifully was blind. The white Connemara seemed to have become almost a symbol of courage in the face of adversity.

Even a daily paper in a nearby city sent over a reporter and a photographer for a story. When it appeared in a Sundy edition the whole supply was quickly sold out in the little village. It was evident that the reporter had forgotten his usual cynicism in the face of Rhonda's honesty and sincerity, for he wrote a sympathetic and understanding story.

He ended by saying: "This is different from most stories of this kind. This young girl is entirely devoted to her pony and has no interest in publicity. So often these stories are planned with one eye on news coverage. This is certainly not the case here. You have only to see the girl and pony together to realize that they almost live in a world of their own. The girl is the pony's eyes and he trusts her completely.

"It seems to me that more than a ribbon should go to such courage and dedication. Perhaps a fund could be started that would buy a fitting trophy for such an outstanding accomplishment. I would be glad to make the first donation."

The Blind Connemara Fund, as it was called, grew quickly. The story evidently had moved many people, for donations of all denominations came in, some obviously from those in limited circumstances and many from children. In a week the fund had reached a total of several hundred dollars and a very handsome silver cup was purchased to be awarded at the Tri-State Show. It was engraved "The Blind Connemara Trophy" and a picture of it appeared in the paper a week before the show. Rhonda was thrilled when she saw it. So was Tim Malley. But Rhonda was also a little worried.

"Won't it look as if it's all arranged for us to win? The trophy named for the pony and all. I don't want it to seem like that."

"Not with that judge there," said Tim Malley. "Everybody knows he's the best and fairest there is. And your pony would win anywhere the way he's going. I've been with horses all my life and I never saw a better performance. When he wins everybody there is going to know he earned it. He'll be out by himself."

Rhonda felt better. She knew how honest and straightforward Tim Malley was.

"It's just that it's all gotten so much bigger and more important than I thought it would be," she said. "I just wanted the pony to win. I didn't know about all these other things."

"These things happen," said Tim Malley. "When people get interested things get blown up. If it's real like this one it doesn't hurt. People like stories like this. If they have problems they like to hear about things like this pony. It makes them feel good."

"You don't think people will think I'm trying to get my picture in the papers and all that, do you?" she asked anxiously.

"That man from the paper didn't think so and nobody who reads what he wrote will, either. If I were you, I'd only worry about getting the pony ready for the show. And not too much about that, either. I don't see how he can miss."

The days were full for Rhonda. She had talked to Tim Malley about getting the pony in top shape.

"You have only to see the girl and pony together
to realize that they almost live in a world of their own.
The girl is the pony's eyes and he trusts her completely."

"His gaits are perfect," he had said. "As smooth as they can possibly be and you can't fault them. His jumping is good, he always jumps big and clean. About the only thing you can work on is trying to get him hard and fit, in perfect condition. Even if such condition isn't called for in a class like that—they only walk, trot and canter a little—judges like to see a horse in really fit condition. They will always pick him over the sleek fat ones. I'd give him a lot of work across country and that will give him an extra edge over most of the others."

So each day they covered many miles and the white pony grew hard and fit. The muscles played under his white coat, which shone with condition. Even when he moved at a slow pace you were aware of the power that could be called on if needed. When he went into a canter it was so smooth and effortless you felt he could keep it up forever.

Each day Rhonda finished the day with a few jumps. As Pony grew more fit he put even more power into them. Now he always cleared the bar with at least a foot to spare. He seemed to glory in the feeling of jumping again.

As the day of the Tri-State Show drew near Rhonda knew he was as fit as a pony could possibly be. She felt sure that nothing could possibly beat him.

16   THE BREAKDOWN

Rhonda was up early grooming the pony. On this day of days she wanted him to look his very best. When she had finished the pony shone, a gleaming white from head to foot. His tail and mane were flowing and silky and his head was high. He seemed to know this was a very special day. Of course he should know, for Rhonda had told him all about it as she worked over him. She always talked to him when she was with him because he seemed to like to hear the tone of her voice. Lately she had begun to have a strange feeling that he understood a great deal of what she was saying. In some ways she felt sure she communicated with him—maybe not with words but with mood and feeling.

Her father and mother were driving them to the show in a small trailer that hitched on behind their car. It was fifty miles away and they wanted to go slowly to give the pony an easy ride, so they were having an early breakfast.

Rhonda was rather excited and did not have much interest in food. But when her father pointed out that the rider should be as fit as his horse, she finally ate her bacon and eggs.

As they rolled along at a leisurely pace through the green countryside Rhonda was thankful for the slight breeze that came through the open front of the trailer. She sat on a stool beside the white pony because she felt he would be happier with her near at hand. Every now and then he put his nose against her shoulder or cheek, seeming to gather comfort from her presence. She was really his only contact with the dark outside world.

It was going to be a hot day and she was glad their class was in the morning. By afternoon the ring, enclosed as it probably was, would be like an oven. Even now she had to mop her forehead occasionally in spite of the breeze that their movement brought through the trailer.

The car stuttered and coughed several times and her father looked concerned. He stepped on the gas as it skipped again and then the engine coughed and stopped. Several times he tried the starter but it would not catch. Rhonda was worried. They were still six miles from the show grounds and they had not too much time to spare for they had made slower time than they had expected. If there was any long delay it would be serious. She had to be on time when her class was called.

Her father opened the hood of the car and looked at the engine but Rhonda knew he was not much of a mechanic. He realized this himself too, for he soon went out and signaled a passing car. When it stopped her father said, "Please stop at the next garage or service station and ask them to send a mechanic out here."

Rhonda led the white pony out of the trailer to let him graze beside the road while they waited. She kept looking at her watch anxiously and watching for the service car but only passenger cars came by. At last she saw a red truck approaching. It came to a stop and a man in coveralls got out. He looked over the engine, then tried to start it with no success. He checked several things and then shook his head.

"The carburetor is shot and if it can be repaired it will be a long job. You'd better get a new one."

"Have you got one?" asked Rhonda's father.

"I'm not sure if I have the right type," said the man. "If not I'll have to run into town to get it."

"How long do you think it will take?" asked Rhonda anxiously.

"Maybe an hour, maybe two," said the man. "I'll do the best I can."

"My daughter has her pony entered in a class at the show that is very important to her. Please hurry it as much as you can. We haven't much time to spare."

"I'll do the best I can," repeated the man as he drove off.

The minutes ticked away as Rhonda watched for his return. At last she realized she could wait no longer.

"I'll have to ride Pony the rest of the way or we'll never make it in time," she said to her parents. "Stand now," she said to the white pony as she went to get the saddle and bridle. As soon as she was saddled up, she swung up and gathered up the reins.

"Watch out for the traffic," her father warned, "and

stay on the grass at the edge of the road as much as you can."

"I'll be careful," said Rhonda as she swung the pony into a slow canter toward the city six miles away. She had an hour before the time for her class and now she was especially glad she had gotten the pony so hard and fit with those long rides. He would need all that strength now.

17   THE LONG RIDE

The Connemara's canter was smooth and seemingly effortless, but the sun was very hot and before long his white coat began to darken with sweat. Everyone driving by looked curiously at the girl cantering along on the white pony. Occasionally someone who thought he was funny called out, "Are the British coming, Miss Revere?" or some such remark, but more often they cheered her, especially if there were children in the car.

Rhonda watched for road signs. When she saw one

that read "4 miles to Northwood," she checked with her watch. They were making good time and should make the class in time if the pony did not tire. Although he was dark with sweat he still felt strong and fresh under her. Occasionally, she pulled him to a walk for a moment, but he seemed anxious to go on and soon resumed his canter. Perhaps he knows the problem, thought Rhonda. He seemed to understand and realize so much more than she had ever thought possible that she was not sure he did not know what all this was about. At the next signpost there was a poster for the Tri-State Show and a sign beneath it, "3 miles to Show Grounds." She was halfway there and still had a little more than a half hour before their class was due.

She had just pulled the pony to a walk for a moment when a big bus pulled up beside them.

"What is the matter?" asked a voice and she recognized the lady from the Sanders Home for Crippled Children.

"Our car broke down," explained Rhonda, "and I was afraid it wouldn't be repaired in time so I'm riding in."

"Won't the poor pony be all tired out?" asked the lady. "He looks so hot and sweaty."

"I think he'll be all right," said Rhonda. "He's

very fit. But it is hot. When you get there please look up Tim Malley and tell him what happened. Maybe he can speak to the people in the ring and explain what happened. They might excuse me if I should be a little late."

"I certainly will, and all good luck," said the lady as the bus drove off. The children all waved and called to her and the pony.

Now Rhonda began watching the white pony very carefully. Although his canter seemed as smooth as ever the miles must have taken something out of him. Still she did not dare to go at a slower pace, for even if everything went well they would only have a few minutes to spare. Perhaps enough to rub him down and give him a few minutes' rest before he went into the ring. She did not think the long ride would affect his performance, but she kept wondering what the judge would think to see her bringing in her pony all dark with sweat. She hoped it wouldn't be held against her. Perhaps she might have a chance to explain. She hoped so.

Now the traffic thickened and she saw a sign, "Tri-State Show 1 mile ahead on left." If her watch was right they still had almost fifteen minutes left before her class would be called. She still did not dare to go slower than a canter but hoped that they could walk the last fifty yards so he would be breathing easily by the time he went into the ring.

At last they saw the Show grounds just ahead and Rhonda felt they could trot and then walk the last part. It would help a little, although the pony was not breathing hard and still seemed fresh. He still carried a high head and looked around at everything with great interest.

The first person she saw was Tim Malley who was hurrying toward her with a pail in one hand and a towel in the other.

"We won't have time to unsaddle and wash him down properly," he said, "but let's do the best we can. He seems all right even after cantering that far. It certainly paid off, giving him all that work to get him in top shape."

He was sponging down the pony all the time, then he got a rub rag and went all over him. Lastly he took the towel and dried the pony as completely as he could. The white pony was still gray, but his wet coat made the play of muscles even more defined. He looked more than ever like a small race horse in top condition.

"He'll do now," said Tim Malley. "Just walk him around until the class is called. And don't worry. He'll go as well as ever. He's in wonderful shape."

18   THE BLIND
CONNEMARA CUP

In a few minutes the call came for entries for the
Ponies Under Saddle Class and the Connemara Cup
to come into the ring. Rhonda rode in, a little worried,
for the pony's wet coat was still far from white. She
looked over and was happy when she saw the gray-
haired judge who had been so kind and understanding
in their first show. He came over to her.

"I was told that your car with trailer broke down
and you had to ride in." He turned to her. "Was it
six miles?"

"I think so," she said. "That's what the signs said."

"And you came at a canter all the way?"

"We had to," said Rhonda. "We only had an hour."

He turned to look at the pony. "He looks fine, except not dry. He must have been in good condition to do that and still come in here like this."

"I think he is," said Rhonda. "Mr. Malley said judges like to see a horse hard and fit even if the class doesn't call for it. So I gave him miles and miles cross country. It seemed to be the only thing to do. To me his trot and canter and jumping were perfect."

"Is Mr. Malley the man who told me about the breakdown?"

"Yes, I guess it must have been. He's always like that, looking out for people."

The judge looked long at the pony and turned away. "Good luck," he said.

Then he turned back. "To be a good judge in anything you have to be fair. You can't let sentiment sway you. If your pony wins today you can be sure it's because he is the best in this class. Even if I like him and you—and I do—it will be like that." And he walked away with his shoulders rigid as if warding off criticism.

The ponies trotted and cantered on command and

Rhonda felt the same lightness of stride. The six-mile ride had not dulled Pony's edge. His walk was as springy and his trot as floating and rhythmic as ever. His canter seemed even better, as if the six miles had been just a workout. Rhonda watched the other ponies but she could not see that any had equaled the Connemara's performance. Then the jump was set up.

The ponies that went first cleared it well enough, for it was not high. But some brushed it and others hesitated and bucked over rather unwillingly. When Pony's turn came she took him up to it and he felt it with his nose. Then he took off in a tremendous leap. Perhaps it seemed too small to him and he wanted something bigger. He jumped it as if it were a foot higher, and with such gaiety that the people at the ringside burst into spontaneous applause.

The judge looked at his card. Then he spoke to the ringmaster, who went to the loud-speaker and said, "The judge wishes to make an announcement before he makes the awards in this class."

Then the judge spoke. "I want to explain that in

He jumped as if it were a foot higher,
and with such gaiety that the people at the ringside
burst into spontaneous applause.

this situation it may seem that sentiment is playing a part in the awards. But I wish to assure everyone that this is not so. The fact that the cup to be given was subscribed to because of interest in a blind pony in this class has had no effect on the judging. Nor has the fact that a breakdown made it necessary for the pony to canter six miles to appear in time. The class was still judged strictly on its merits. The pony awarded the trophy in this class is definitely the best in spite of the handicap of being blind.

"So it gives me great pleasure to award the blue ribbon and the Blind Connemara Trophy to the pony who was responsible for it. He has earned it in every way."

The applause that followed was tremendous. Rhonda's hand shook as she patted the pony's neck.

"We did it," she said. "We really did it."

ABOUT THE AUTHOR

C. W. Anderson grew up in Nebraska and studied at the Art Institute of Chicago before moving to New York City, where he soon developed the interest in horses that came to dominate his life as artist and sportsman.

In 1936 Macmillan published Mr. Anderson's first book, *Billy and Blaze,* the start of a series of easy-to-read picture-storybooks that have sold nearly a million copies over the years. Mr. Anderson also wrote and illustrated many horse stories for older readers, such as *The Outlaw* and *Phantom, Son of the Gray Ghost,* and such treasuries as *Twenty Gallant Horses* and the *Complete Book of Horses and Horsemanship.*

Mr. Anderson divided his time between a small country home in Mason, New Hampshire, and a studio in Boston. He was working in Boston on the illustrations for *The Blind Connemara* at the time of his death in the spring of 1971.